NOV - - 2009

Dog and Bear

THREE TO GET READY

Laura Vaccaro Seeger

A NEAL PORTER BOOK
ROARING BROOK PRESS
NEW YORK

For my brothers, Billy and Tommy

A Neal Porter Book

Published by Roaring Brook Press

Roaring Brook Press is a division of Holtzbrinck Publishing Holdings Limited Partnership

175 Fifth Avenue, New York, New York 10010

www.roaringbrookpress.com

Distributed in Canada by H. B. Fenn and Company, Ltd.

Cataloging-in-Publication Data is on file at the Library of Congress

ISBN-13: 978-1-59643-396-0

ISBN-10: 1-59643-396-5

Roaring Brook Press books are available for special promotions and premiums.
For details, contact: Director of Special Markets, Holtzbrinck Publishers.

Book design by Jennifer Browne

Printed in China

First edition September 2009

2 4 6 8 10 9 7 5 3 1

uh-oh

"Oh, my."

"Oh, no."

"Bear? is that you?"

"Yes, Dog. I've got a bucket stuck on my head!"

"I can see that, Bear. Let me help you."

"Uh-oh," said Dog.

"Oh, my."

"Oh, no."

"What will I do, DOG? There will be a bucket on my head FOREVER."

"Not to worry, Bear. I know what to do."

"Hooray! You did it!"

"Uh-oh."

oops

"DOG, what are you doing?"

"Look, Bear. I can fly!"

"I am a plane soaring through the clouds!"

"Be careful, Dog," said Bear.

"I AM MASTER OF THE UNIVERSE!"

"Oops," said Dog.
"Now I am a fish in the sea."

"What a mess! Dog needs to be more organized."

"What's the matter, Dog?"

"Oh, Bear. I can't find my sock monkey. I have looked everywhere."

"Don't worry. I have organized all your toys and books and bones and sticks. Just look in the box marked 'C' for 'cuddly.'"

"No sock monkey here," said Dog.

"Oh, I meant 'A' for 'adorable,'" said Bear.
"I don't see it," said Dog.

"Hmm. Try 'F' for 'floppy' . . ."

"Nope," said Dog.

"Oh, no! what have I done? I have lost Dog's sock monkey!"

"It's all right, Bear. I will play with my other toys instead."

"Look, Bear. Here's my sock monkey!"

"Of course. It's in the box
marked 'S' for 'soft,'" said Bear.

"And 'super special,'" said DOG.